TEEN TITANS™
Short-Circuit Chef

by Acton Figueroa

Illustrated by Joe Staton and Mike DeCarlo
Color by Lee Loughridge

Published by Scholastic Inc. SCHOLASTIC and associated logos are trademarks and/or registered trademarks of Scholastic Inc.
ISBN 0-439-78961-3
Designed by Henry Ng and Bethany Dixon

12 11 10 9 8 7 6 5 4 3 2   6 7 8 9 10/0

Printed in the U.S.A.
First printing, April 2006

SCHOLASTIC INC.
New York   Toronto   London   Auckland   Sydney
Mexico City   New Delhi   Hong Kong   Buenos Aires

Late one afternoon, Cyborg was walking back to Titan Tower. He had worked out all morning, and his gigantic cybermuscles were pumped. He was thinking about what he was going to eat when he got home.

He didn't notice that he was being watched.

With a roar, Mammoth pounced on Cyborg. Cyborg pulled his huge arm back to throw a punch, but Jinx did a midair flip and pinned Cyborg's arm to the ground.

Gizmo slipped in and undid a steel plate on Cyborg's side. As Mammoth leaned hard on Cyborg, Gizmo made one quick snip with his pliers, and Cyborg stopped moving.

Cyborg lay very still while Gizmo worked on his wiring.

The next morning, Starfire couldn't find Cyborg. "Where is he?" she asked. "He's usually up by now."

Raven came out of her room. "It *is* late. I wonder where he could be."

Above them, a door slammed, and they heard Cyborg's heavy footsteps on the stairs.

"I'm going to the mall," Cyborg announced. "I've got a new job."

He was almost out the door when Beast Boy caught up with him. "What kind of a job did you get, Cyborg?" Beast Boy asked. "Aren't you already pretty busy fighting crime?"

"I'm making cupcakes at a new fast food place," Cyborg replied. "I have to run!"

While Robin, Starfire, Raven, and Beast Boy ate breakfast, they talked about Cyborg's new job. Robin was curious.

"I think we should go to the mall to check out this cupcake place," he said.

"And we can eat some cupcakes!" joked Beast Boy.

Raven was quiet for a minute. "There was something strange about Cyborg this morning," she said thought-fully. "I don't know what it was, but I think we need to find out more about what he's doing."

At the mall, the Teen Titans didn't have to look very hard to find the cupcake place. They saw a long line of people waiting to use what looked like an automated teller machine. People were putting their bank cards into the slot and punching in their codes.

But instead of dispensing money, the machine was dispensing cupcakes!

"These are the best cupcakes I've ever eaten!" one woman raved.

Robin watched as everyone gobbled their cupcake up right away.

"Hey," said Beast Boy. "How do we get to Cyborg?"

The Teen Titans searched and found a small door.

Right in the center of it all, Cyborg was connected to cables running from every corner of the room. The Teen Titans could see that his cyberkinetic circuitry was controlling the entire cupcake making and selling process. "Something is wrong here!" Raven whispered.

Raven was right. Something *was* wrong! The cupcake bakery was being run by the HIVE. Gizmo, Mammoth, and Jinx were watching the Teen Titans on closed-circuit TV from a small room behind the kitchen.

Gizmo slammed down his fist. "We can't let the Teen Titans mess up our mission!"

Jinx giggled. "Don't worry, Gizmo. Most of the people in the mall have already eaten our mind-control cupcakes. They'll do whatever we want. Soon the whole city will be under our control, and then the Teen Titans won't be able to stop us!"

"What should we do?" Starfire asked Robin as the Teen Titans walked through the mall.

Before Robin could answer, a little boy ran right into Beast Boy and almost knocked him down.

Beast Boy bent down to look at the little boy. "Hey, kid," he said gently, "you should be more careful. You might hurt yourself."

The little boy's mouth was smeared with cupcake frosting. "Hey, mister," he growled, "the only one around here who is going to get hurt is you!" With that, he kicked Beast Boy in the knee.

"Ow!" Beast Boy yelled.

The Teen Titans looked around. The normally peaceful mall had changed. People were arguing, shouting, and fighting.

Little old ladies were cutting in line. Kids were tipping over mannequins. Mothers were shoving other mothers to get to the sale racks. And every single person they saw had cupcake frosting on his or her face.

"I don't know what's going on, but I think the cupcakes must have something to do with it," Robin said. "Let's go talk to Cyborg!"

SALE!

19

At the bakery, the line was twice as long as before. "I saw some of these people in line earlier," Raven said. "There's something bad in those cupcakes. It's making people act evil!"

"Excuse me," Robin said to the people in line. "Hey, listen up! I don't think you people should be eating so many cupcakes. Umm . . . too much sugar is bad for your teeth!"

"Go away!" yelled an old man. A toddler in a stroller threw his bottle at Robin.

"Ouch!" Robin cried. "That hurt!"

"We'd better find Cyborg!" Beast Boy said.

The Teen Titans stepped into the kitchen. Cyborg was even busier now than before. Thousands of cupcakes were stacked on high racks, the mixers were mixing furiously, and the ovens glowed from the heat.

As Raven stepped inside, the door slammed shut behind her. Mammoth, Gizmo, and Jinx stepped out from behind it.

The Teen Titans were trapped!

With a roar, Mammoth hurled himself at Robin. Gizmo launched jet rockets at Starfire and Raven. And Jinx and Beast Boy began a crazy fight, with Jinx somersaulting in midair and Beast Boy shape-shifting from boy to bat and back again.

Through it all, Cyborg just kept working on his cupcakes.

Mammoth used his amazing strength to slam Robin into an oven. Starfire and Raven struggled to avoid the flares of Gizmo's rockets.

As Jinx and Beast Boy fought, Beast Boy called out to Cyborg. "C'mon, man, help us here!" he cried. "We're getting creamed!"

Cyborg glanced at Beast Boy for a second. "I wish I could," he said. "I *really* wish I could. But I can't stop making these cupcakes."

Beast Boy noticed that Cyborg looked like he was about to overheat!

Hmm, thought Beast Boy. *I wonder what would happen if —*"Yooooow!" he screamed.

Jinx had caught him by the ankles and was spinning him around and around. Then, suddenly, she let go! Beast Boy crashed into a gigantic mixing bowl of frosting.

With a splash and a sizzle, a huge glob of frosting landed right on Cyborg's overheated circuit board.

Everyone in the kitchen stopped to look at Cyborg as he sparked and smoked and spun around, ripping out all of the cables.

Cyborg looked around and noticed Mammoth holding Robin in a head lock.

"Hey," Cyborg shouted. "Let go of my friend!"

Cyborg jumped into the fight, and within minutes the Teen Titans had cornered the HIVE.

"Don't come any closer!" Gizmo said.

Before anyone could move, Gizmo detonated a small, round bomb that smoked and fizzled and filled the kitchen with a thick, smelly fog. When the smoke had cleared, the HIVE members were gone.

The Teen Titans had won! They threw away all of the cupcakes and wheeled the kitchen equipment out with the trash.

Without a fresh supply of cupcakes, the people in the mall slowly returned to normal. The Titans had saved the day again.

Back at the Tower, everyone sat around talking about the evil cupcake caper.

Finally, Starfire changed the subject. "Cyborg, I'm hungry," she said. "Do you think you could make us something to eat? We all know you can cook."

Cyborg stood up and headed into the kitchen. "What are you hungry for?" he asked. "I'll make anything except cupcakes!"